Hmmm... I get it!

You **actually** meant to turn the page the other way to close the book, **didn't you?**

Well, you've accidentally gone further in.

Oh! You again. Well, you'll notice I'm back to being little, old, non-rabbity, normal me. So, no point reading on because this book is **very, very** boring.

WHAT ARE YOU DOING?

We've just gone over this.

As I mentioned before, there is **nothing** to see in this book.

Everything is perfectly **normal** so **please** don't turn the page **again**.

EEEEK! You've done it again.

OKAY, let's just talk about this. I'll put my washing away and then we can discuss it, monster to human.

In the meantime, **please don't**
turn the page
again.

Brrrrr...

It's getting **chilly**
in this book, isn't it?

*(That's the only reason I've
put all these clothes on.)*

You better close it up before you catch a **cold**.

For the sake of your own health, **please don't** turn the page again.

Just joking! It's not really that cold and I didn't need that jacket anyway.

ANYHOO...

as I said, this is a really **boring** book because I'm just relaxing today.

I'm doing nothing, so there's **no point in turning** the page again.

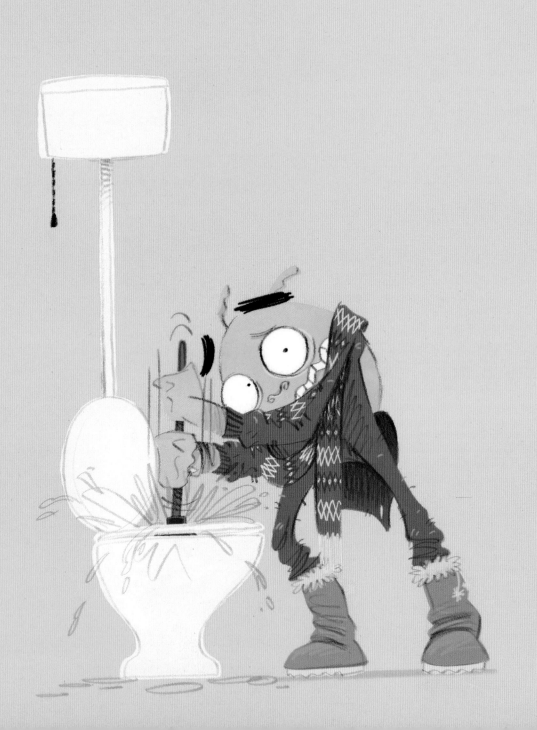

I don't know if you've noticed it,
but I'm telling you...
PLEASE DON'T TURN THE PAGE AGAIN!

GOOD GRIEF!

You're not STOPPING. Do you realise that every time you turn the page my clothes disappear?

That's why I ask you, for the sake of a little **PRIVACY**...

PLEASE DON'T TURN THE PAGE AGAIN.

You silly duffer! You've got the book upside down... turn it around.

That's better. Now feel free to
read all the way to the end of the book.
Go for it. Please turn the page again.

Drat! I tried to trick you into thinking the book
went the other way. You are too smart for me.

I'm begging though...

please don't turn the page
again.

Golly gosh! You cannot be STOPPED.

Wow! Look at this beautiful painting...

I hear you can look at it for 1,000 hours and never get bored. I guess you'll **never** turn the page again.

Okay... this is it.
It's just you, me and
my underpants.

I'm confident you'll
do the right thing.

Please, please, PLEASE DON'T turn the page AGAIN.

Can someone **please** pass me the **sunscreen?**